Daddy-Care

Story Allen Morgan
Illustrations John Richmond

862169

Annick Press Ltd.
Toronto, Canada, M2N 5S3

Copyright © 1986 Allen Morgan (Text)
Copyright © 1986 John Richmond (Art)

Annick Press gratefully acknowledges the contributions of
The Canada Council and The Ontario Arts Council

Canadian Cataloguing in Publication Data

Morgan, Allen, 1946–
  Daddy-care

ISBN 0-920303-58-7 (bound). — ISBN 0-920303-59-5 (pbk.)

I. Richmond, John, 1926–   II. Title.

PS8576.073D32 1986   jC813'.54   C86-093069-6
PZ7.M67Da 1986

Distributed in Canada and the U.S.A. by: Firefly Books Ltd.

Printed and bound in Canada by D.W. Friesen & Sons,
Altona, Manitoba

*For Kimberly, Kaleigh and
their First-Prize Daddy*

On Monday morning the alarm didn't work, so Danny and his Dad woke up at a quarter to eight. When Danny saw the time he was a little worried. He knew they'd be late if they didn't hurry.

"Come on!" he called to his Dad. "We've got to get up and get going!"

But Danny's Dad didn't seem to want to go anywhere at all. It took him a while to put on his socks and even longer to do up his shirt. Then, when it was time to put on his shoes, he lost one of them and Danny had to help him look for it.

"Please don't dilly dally," Danny told him.

Danny's Dad promised to go a little faster, but even so he took an awfully long time to eat his breakfast. He played with his eggs and he told Danny that the coffee was too hot and he could only drink it in little sips. Danny didn't say anything but he had the feeling that his Dad might be going slow on purpose.

On the way to daycare Danny's Dad was just as bad. He stopped twice to tie his shoes and he kept on losing his newspaper. He even dropped his lunch a couple of times and when they finally got to daycare he grabbed Danny's arm and he wouldn't let go.

"Why are you going away?" he said. "Can't you stay?"

Danny was very patient. He explained to his Dad that he had a very hard day coming up at school and he had to go now if he wanted to be on time.

"But when are you coming back?" asked his Dad.

"At four o'clock this afternoon," said Danny. "Just like always."

Then Danny left. His Dad watched from the window and waved goodbye. He was feeling a little sad and he almost cried, but the teacher came by and gave him something to play with instead.

Danny's Dad didn't stay sad for long. There were many other dads at daycare that day and plenty of good things to do. Larry had a new convertible for show-and-tell, and Stan brought in his van. Brad had one of his semis there too, so they all decided to go out in the back alley and customize them for a while.

"How do you like those Blue Jays?" said Stan as he jacked up his van. "I bet they go all the way this year!"

"You better believe it," said Danny's Dad. "Toronto's going to win the World Series, no problem."

"Hey, I used to play a little baseball myself," said Larry. "I bet I could've made the Jays for sure if I'd have only tried."

All the other guys agreed that they could have played in the big leagues too.

When it was time for lunch everyone came in and washed their hands. Then they all sat down and took out their sandwiches.

"Hey, alright!" said Larry. "I got corned beef! What did you guys get?"

"Salami!" said Stan.

"Ham and swiss on rye!" said Brad.

"Peanut butter and jelly," said Danny's Dad, and he wasn't too happy about it. He had peanut butter and jelly almost every day. Larry agreed to sell him something better, but he said it would cost three cookies and half an apple.

"That's too much," complained Danny's Dad.

"Hey, what can I say?" said Larry. "If you wanna eat corned beef, it's gonna cost."

Danny's Dad glared at Larry but he didn't say anything. He made the trade. Corned beef was his favourite.

"A guy could starve with a lunch like this," he said to himself. "Why don't I ever get something good like the other guys do?"

Then, just to get even, Danny's Dad took a bite out of each of the cookies when Larry wasn't looking. Larry didn't catch him but he knew who to blame. When Danny's Dad was pouring his coffee, Larry bumped his arm and made him spill most of it. The teacher didn't see how it happened, so Danny's Dad had to clean it up all by himself, even though it wasn't his fault. It made him mad. For a minute it looked like there might be a fight, but the teacher came by.

"Nap time," she said and she took out the cots. All the dads liked taking naps a lot, so it wasn't very long before everyone was fast asleep.

Danny didn't have a nap. School started again right after lunch, so he had to go back to his classroom instead. Danny worked very hard all that afternoon, but every so often he stopped for a moment and thought about his Dad.

"I wonder how he's doing today," he said to himself. "I hope he's having a good time."

Danny's Dad woke up from his nap before the other dads, so he checked in the newspaper to see how his stocks were doing, and then he read the funnies. When nap time was over he got out the cards and everyone played poker for a while. Larry was the one who won most of the money. He spread out his cards and said, "Read 'em and weep!", and no-one could keep him from sweeping the pots.

"How come you've got six cards and I only have five?" said Danny's Dad.

"The dealer always gets an extra one," Larry told him.

"Does not," said Danny's Dad. "That's not the way you're supposed to play poker!"

"Is too!" yelled Larry.

"Is not, no way!" Danny's Dad yelled back and they had a fight about it.

The teacher made them sit in the corner and later on, when Danny came by to pick up his Dad, she told him what happened.

Danny's Dad tried to explain over dinner.

"Larry's the one who started it all. It was all his fault," he said.

"Are you sure that's true?" Danny asked his Dad. "It takes two to argue, you know."

"Maybe so but with Larry it just takes one," said his Dad. "Larry's a creep!"

"He is?" said Danny and he sounded surprised. "I thought Larry was your best friend."

"So did I," said his Dad. "But he's not any more."

"Sometimes even best friends get mad at each other," Danny told his Dad. "Why, I'll bet Larry feels just as bad as you do."

"You really think so?" asked his Dad.

"Absolutely," said Danny. "So when you see him tomorrow, why don't you tell him you're sorry you yelled and you don't want to fight any more. He might just feel the same way as you do, and if he does, then you and he can be best friends again, alright?"

Danny's Dad said he would try and he promised not to fight at daycare any more. Then he went upstairs to watch the news on T.V. while Danny did the dishes.

Then Danny's Dad had his bath, he brushed his teeth and got ready for bed. Danny was very busy with his homework, so his Dad had to do it all by himself.

Then it was time for Danny's Dad to go to sleep. Danny came in and read him a story, he sang him a song and it wasn't long before it was time to turn out the light.

"Good night, Dad," said Danny. "Sleep tight."

"Good night," said his Dad. "I'm really glad that we live here together."

"So am I," said Danny and he gave his Dad a great big hug.